D1452647

A Tyrant's Wrath

By Jordan Blaise

This is a work of fiction. Names, characters, places, and incidents either are the product of the author's imagination or are used fictitiously. Any resemblance to actual persons, living or dead, events, or locales is completely coincidental.

Copyright © 2021 by Jordan Blaise

All rights reserved. No part of this book may be reproduced or used in any manner without written permission of the copyright owner except for the use of quotations in book review.

First paperback edition May 2021

Book cover design by Robin Johnson

ISBN 978-0-578-92552-3 (Ebook)

ISBN 978-0-578-92553-0 (Paperback)

PREFACE

This book came into being at first from an idea as I was watching a documentary. That idea rolled like a snowball into planning, organizing, plotting, drafting, editing, and hard work. Wrath is a hard thing for many, so I wanted to create a book to relate to those suffering in the projects who are dealing with wrath due to their circumstances, loss of a loved one, family issues, or other things. However, in no way, shape, or form with this book am I encouraging gang activity or saying that there is no hope for those in the hood, this story simply follows the characters' decisions and feelings. With that said, this book wouldn't be possible without the One guiding me and helping me persevere to complete it, Jehovah. I also must thank my mother and father for putting in a great effort to help make my dream come true. I give my thanks, as well, to Craig Gibb and Phil Marcelin over at Story Perfect Editing Services, they did their best to make my story reach its utmost potential. Also, thanks to Robin Johnson from Robin Ludwig Design Inc. this book cover was made possible. Thank you all, this has been a journey.

PROLOGUE

"Tyrant gang for life!"

My brother said that all the time. I was sitting on the couch of our apartment, watching a gang movie as my brother was practicing Tyrant signs.

Tomorrow I'd be joining the Tyrants. Tyreek, my brother, was in that gang, and he was the coolest person I've ever known. Ma always said that Tyreek was just like dad, the same smile, the same charismatic energy, too bad dad left us and was locked up in prison, at least that's what my mom told me.

"Sean, come over here and do these dishes!" she said.

"Ma, I'm watchin' a movie. I'll do 'em after," I said.

"Boy, if you don't do them damn dishes."

I sighed at my mom's reply and walked over to our

kitchen sink.

As I was doing the dishes I thought about what tomorrow would be like. I'd finally join the Tyrants. But this wasn't really about being like Tyreek, it was about the power. I could be popular at school, I would be respected, and I could be strong. I wouldn't have to depend on Tyreek anymore. But, I wouldn't complain about spending more time with him.

I finished washing the last dish and dried the kitchen sink with an old rag. Couches and air mattresses were the only things we slept on, and some days we'd only have one meal. This was the only life I've ever known, these projects.

I sat back down on the tattered couch and continued my movie. Just twenty minutes passed when Tyreek said, "C'mon, we goin' to Dwayne's house."

"No, lemme finish my movie!"

"Bruh, if you don't get up!" Tyreek sounded just like our mom.

I sighed. "Fine, let's go." Dwayne was our cousin, the shot caller of the Tyrants.

We walked through the streets of Sacktown. I looked at my brother in the radiant sunlight. He had his curly afro going for him, he wasn't skinny but he was a bit slim. That was normal though, since he ran track.

As we were walking, we saw some Tyrants chilling by the local corner store, Fyre's.

"Yo, wassup, gang?" Tyreek said.

"We just chillin', dog, enjoying the environment with all this cash from our sales!" one of them said, I assumed he was talking about their drug sales. I hoped to make that kind of cash one day, we'd have more food in the fridge.

Another asked "Ayo, where y'all going?"

"Over to Sergeant D's, man!" Tyreek replied. The whole gang called Dwayne that so he wouldn't get in trouble with the cops. But Tyreek said it all the time just as a joke because Dwayne always barked orders to the Tyrants.

We walked away and a Tyrant called to me "Ayo, good luck tomorrow!"

I looked back and gave him a head's up, I was going to need that luck.

Tyreek and I arrived at Dwayne's red painted suburban house, only the shot caller of the Tyrants could have such a good house like this. All of us chilled as we watched television. Compared to Tyreek, Dwayne was pretty quiet, stroking his growing mustache often. Dwayne was twenty-three, and he always acted so mature. His low fade and stud earrings went well with his lighter complexion. He mostly talked about business of the gang, and there's something about him that makes you want to follow his orders.

After we chilled for a bit Dwayne asked me, "So, are you ready for tomorrow?"

"I was born ready," I said, but I didn't really mean it. I wanted to be a Tyrant, but I didn't want to get locked up, or worse, die! I was scared, but I've been waiting too long not to join.

"Yeah, that's my brother right there!" Tyreek said. Dwayne chuckled with Tyreek. I couldn't let them down.

My entire life as long as I could remember has revolved around the Tyrants, whether it was hanging around them with Tyreek or practicing Tyrant gang signs. And now, I was finally able to join. It was unfair that the only option society presented me still formed a mountain of fear inside.

Tyreek and I left Dwayne's house from Stream-ville and went home to our small apartment. I sat back on the couch and finished my movie, it was good. But I hoped that I wouldn't end up like some of the characters.

The next day Tyreek and I went outside to meet with the rest of the Tyrants. The summer sun was beam-ing, which didn't help my fearful sweating at all. Five minutes felt like ten seconds how fast dozens of Tyr-ants gathered up. We were in Dwayne's grassy back-yard, with a large wooden fence blocking anyone's outside view.

Dwayne got all of their attention by walking up to me. "Sean, to become a Tyrant, you have to beat up one of us."

Seriously? I'd have to win in a fight against one of these guys, some of the most ruthless guys in Sack-town?!

"Oh, and you don't choose who you fight, we do," Dwayne said. I nodded, but everyone surely knew I was scared by how wide my eyes grew. "Ray, come over here!"

Someone came out from the crowd, his lean physique and cornrows let me know he was Ray. Damn, he had the best hands in Sacktown, his dad literally owned a boxing gym! Even though I had a couple of fights in school and stuff, this guy was on a different level.

"You ready little boy?" Ray said. He was wearing a white tank top and some shorts, he had boxing gloves too.

"Wassup with the gloves?" I asked. Dwayne gave me a pair of boxing gloves.

"No kicking, only punching, now put them gloves on and start the fight!" Dwayne said. I put the gloves on and everyone backed up. Hopefully all my re-watches of Rocky would come in handy. Ray held his hand out, we touched gloves and the fight began.

Ray started swinging at me and all I could do was block. He threw an unexpected punch at my ribcage, which disrupted my balance as he threw a left swing. I got knocked down but swiftly got up. I heard every-one in the crowd oohing and Tyreek saying, "Come on Sean, get him!"

It was then that I remembered what I was there for, to be a Tyrant.

Ray threw a right hook, but I swiftly ducked. There was my chance! I uppercutted Ray so fast and so hard that he fell down from the air, flat on his back!

I won! The Tyrants were cheering for me! I took my gloves off and helped Ray up. Ray just walked off without a word, avoiding the crowd's gazes.

Dwayne came up to me, "Congrats, Sean, you're a Tyrant now. Are you ready for this lifestyle, man?" I nodded. Dwayne patted me on the back.

Little did I know that I could never be ready for a lifestyle like this, ever.

CHAPTER 1

It's been a few months since I've become a Tyrant, and things were, for the most part, cool.

The other Tyrants taught me everything they did and how they did it. I learned how to steal, pick-pocket, run from the cops (Tyreek was the best at that), fight, carjack, etc. I felt like I knew everything, but I didn't, I wasn't even close. Whenever I got too cocky, someone always put me in my place.

Tyreek and I walked to our school, Rosewall High, probably the worst school in Toussaint County. Most of the students didn't care about it, and half of the teachers didn't either. But as a freshman the school was still pretty new, after all, it was only November.

On our way to school, we met up with Ray. Tyreek and Ray did their smooth handshake and I was left hanging. Ever since I uppercutted Ray in the summer he's had beef with me. We couldn't fight or argue because of my brother in the way, so Ray just ignored me.

We walked through Sacktown, all three of us. We did this every day so that nobody could try anything on our way to school, particularly the Sackers.

The Sacker gang were our rivals. I've encountered some of them before, but they've always cowered away because I'd be with other Tyrants.

Tyreek, Ray and I arrived at school after talking about new hip-hop music and the last football game.

"Ayo, I gotta get to class man," Ray said.

"Aight, see ya after school then," replied Ty.

"Yeah, see ya!" said Ray, leaving. My brother and I walked through the crowded hallways, where many others would make room for us. The perks of being a Tyrant.

"Yo, Ty," only I could call him that, "you think our football team is gonna win tomorrow?"

"Hell yeah! Ray and them know what they doin'!" said Tyreek, with his usual high level of energy. Ty was always hyped.

"I dunno, man, they goin' against Streamville tomorrow, I heard they're undefeated!"

"Well, we'll see tomorrow. Catch you later, Sean."

"Peace," I replied as we left for our own classes.

In the middle of math class I was talking to some other Tyrants.

"I got my eyes on Patricia man, she cute!" said CJ, sitting in a desk behind mine. He was a junior, but he was pretty dumb. CJ was hefty and bulky as the football team's linebacker.

"Oh, I see you like vanilla, CJ!" I said.

"What, I can't like a white girl?" asked CJ.

"I don't know what's wrong with dating a white girl," said Devon to my right. Devon's been my friend since elementary. He was a freshman, like me. Devon wasn't a Tyrant though, he'd spend his time reading books or some other nerdy stuff. But since we were so close he hung out with me and other Tyrants at times, even though his dad was a Sacker. We made sure to keep that under wraps, for his safety and mine.

"Yeah, okay Devon. Man, you wish you could get any girl with them nerdy glasses!" said CJ.

"C'mon, man, you ain't gotta do Devon like that." I said.

"Whatever, man." replied CJ. "I just hope she sees me destroyin' in the football game."

"I wouldn't get your hopes up with a chick during the game." said Devon.

"Ayo what's dat 'posed to mean?" CJ asked with a temper.

"What I mean is that the team our school's going against might not make tomorrow such a pleasant game," Devon explained.

"Man, with me on the team our defense is flawless!" defended CJ.

"My brother Ty said that y'all got the dub," I said. "But I've gotta agree with Devon for this one."

"Whatever, man! I'm just tryna do dis mathwork. If I fail this damn class again, I'll have to repeat a grade!" replied CJ. We all agreed and continued with our math.

Later that day, after walking with Tyreek and Ray, we arrived at Dwayne's house. Other Tyrants (besides me and Tyreek) didn't usually go to hang out at Dwayne's house because he didn't want them over. But today was special.

We all greeted Dwayne and entered his living room where we saw CJ with a girl and two other Tyrants on the red sofa chilling. The house smelled like weed, and the loud music from a boombox inside made the meeting feel like a cookout.

Tyreek, with his usual booming energy, asked "Who's ready to get high?"

"Of course, man!" said one of the Tyrants.

"Hell yeah!" said the girl sitting on CJ's lap.

Everyone seemed excited except for Jason, a quiet Latino Tyrant chilling in a corner. He had his usual durag on, nothing as a top, and a ripped body. Jason was a big and bad Tyrant who killed people who were on the Tyrants' bad side. Different than murder actually, it was more like assassination, or at least that's how other Tyrants described it. Counting Jason's tattoos would be difficult, but he didn't have any on his face, probably so he wouldn't be too recognizable.

"A'ight, I got all this weed, so let's make it happen!" replied Tyreek, with his slick smile that indicated he was about to have some fun! Tyreek really shouldn't have been smoking when he was trying to be a track star, but I kept to myself. Tyreek wouldn't care anyway.

Tyreek and Ray shared a joint with everyone except for me and Dwayne. Dwayne told me to never get high even if my life depended on it. I didn't know why he didn't want me to have fun with everyone else, but I never protested against him.

I chilled with the Tyrants for a bit. At first there wasn't much talking, but I think the weed kicked into them later when they were all droll. The only people who weren't hyperly having fun were me, Dwayne, and Jason.

In the midst of everyone getting high and having fun, Dwayne pulled me over to another room of his house and shut the door.

"Wassup, man?" I asked.

"Sean, I've been thinking, man," he said as he stroked his thin mustache. "The Tyrants have been slackin' lately. They just been smokin' weed, and that gets 'em off task. We ain't getting enough sales! Sure, stealing has brought us a long way, but we can't survive just off of dat!"

I understood his point, the Tyrants haven't been able to steal much lately because a lot of people have been staying home. "So, what are you going to do?" I asked.

"You mean, what are *we* gonna do?"

"What does this have to do with me? What can I do?"

"You think that we took you under our wing and taught you our Tyrant ways for nothing?" I didn't know how to respond to that. After I became a Tyrant in the summer, the whole gang has protected me and taught me a lot. The one who taught me the most though was Dwayne. "I need someone to help me manage everything, to make sure that our dealing is going well."

"I don't know, isn't there anyone better for the job than a rookie like me?'

"C'mon, Sean, don't be a buster! Why do you think I gave you the opportunity to be a Tyrant? It wasn't just 'cuz you're my cousin, Sean, I knew you could get us some serious paper. Now, did I think wrong, are you actually a coward?" asked Dwayne.

I wasn't a coward. "A'ight man, I'm down."

"Good, meet me next week. I'll see you then."

We walked out of the room to see the Tyrants dancing to music from the loud television.

"Yo, Sergeant D, what did y'all talk about?" asked Tyreek.

"Nothin'," Dwayne said.

The next day I met up with other Tyrants at the football game. The Tyrants that were there mostly went to Rosewall High, but some snuck in to watch.

I sat next to Tyreek, and a few other Tyrants were behind us. The teams finished warming up and the game finally began.

"We'll see if Streamville stays undefeated or not," said Tyreek.

"I'm cheering for Rosewall either way!" I replied.

We cheered like crazy that game, and Ray (as running back) actually juked Streamville out for most of the game, and barely any of Streamville's people could get past CJ! Our team won 56–14!

"Yo, I'ma hang with the gang, man, tell ma I'll be okay, aight." said Ty as we exited the school.

"A'ight, man," I said.

Most times when I walked home or to school, Ty was with me. But sometimes he'd leave to hang out with other Tyrants and do crazy stuff. I guess I understood what Dwayne meant by "immature".

I was about halfway home in the dark night when I heard faint footsteps. I glanced behind me and saw three guys in hoods just a block away. I increased my pace and glanced back after a few steps; they were walking faster.

I panicked as my heart skipped a beat and my mind spun through dozens of scenarios, they were probably Sackers looking for a fight! I was reluctant to run because they may have had guns, but it was my best option.

I heard one of them mumble, "Ayo let's sack this fool!"

With that I broke off from the route to my house and took a right to a new block. I ran for my life, they may not have had guns, but one of them definitely at least had a knife if they were trying to fight.

"Hurry, don't let him get away!" ordered one of the Sackers.

I ran as fast as I could, but the Sackers chasing me were definitely more fit.

I turned into an alley and made a left onto a different block. I was starting to get tired and one Sacker was trailing me by about five yards.

I tried to be unpredictable by swerving left to right as I ran but to no avail. With three older guys chasing me, I was dead meat. One Sacker eventually caught up to me and yanked me by my hood. My balance shifted and I fell to the pavement.

The Sacker kicked my arms as I tried to defend myself. I looked into the Sacker's dark eyes, but I couldn't fully memorize his face as the two others caught up and started stomping me. The harsh sounds of their shoes battering my body was all I could hear then.

I wailed; was I going to die? I gasped for air as my arm cracked with a hard kick. I thought that I was strong and cool since I was a Tyrant who knocked out the best boxer in Sacktown, but without others helping me, I didn't mean anything. No one protected me, not even my big brother.

Tears streamed from my eyes. "Tyrant scum!" one said. "Take that! Sackers for life!" another said.

I eventually heard a police siren in the distance. "Ayo dip, dip!" a Sacker said, they left me to rot. I couldn't get up, the burning pain throughout my body didn't let me.

The Sackers were long gone when the police arrived. Two cops picked me up and slammed my head against their car. I winced as they aggressively frisked me and then cuffed me, saying, "You have the right to remain silent, anything you say may be used against you in a—"

"I didn't do nothin', man! I didn't do nothin'! People jumped me man!" I pleaded, interrupting them.

"Shut the fuck up!" a cop said as he pressed my face into the car. "You Tyrant scum should all be locked away." They didn't help my pain as they shoved me into the car.

The Tyrant gang didn't make me invincible, it never could. I cried and looked out of the tinted window as they drove me to the police station. This was a nightmare, straight from the depths of Sacktown's hood.

CHAPTER 2

There I was at the police station with my face buried in my hands. I wondered if I was going to court, or even jail!

I was sitting down in a chair of a dark gray room, facing a wretched cop. Earlier they allowed me to call an appropriate adult, my mom, to be with me as they searched me and recorded my name, address, and fingerprints. That whole time my mom didn't speak with me, as if I was a stranger to her, as if she was ashamed to have me as her child.

"How are you today," my interviewer looked through his paper, "Mr. Sean Harper?"

"It's not like you care," I said under my breath.

The cop shook his head and continued with his questions. "Have you been interacting with any drugs, like meth or cocaine?"

"No, man! You can ask the cops who took me here, they found me on the ground! Some guys came and beat me up when I was walking home," I said aggressively.

"Where were you coming from?" he asked.

"The school football game," I said.

"Hmm… Is there anything else you'd like to confess?"

"Confess!? Look, I'm innocent, okay! You should be looking for the guys who did this to me!"

"Alright, we'll see once I speak with your mom. You can leave now," said the cop. I immediately got up and went out of the interview room door, where my mom was waiting. She straightened her symmetrical bob of hair and didn't make any eye contact with me as she walked into the interview room, shutting the door behind her.

I waited outside of the interview room, thinking of the possible outcomes that could happen to me. Incarceration, fines, probation! My mind was racing as my hands shook uncontrollably.

If I got locked up would I be able to finally see my dad?

I looked at the cop watching me, my shaky hands turned into clenched fists. I couldn't help but be upset at everything that was going on. I gritted my teeth harshly, thinking of different ways I could get revenge.

Anger issues never lost me, it hasn't since I was told the story about how my dad left.

The interview room door finally opened up. "Sean, you're free to go. There's no solid evidence of you doing anything wrong, but we'll be watching you. So do the right thing," the interview cop said, but I didn't pay him any mind. My mom and I left the station, and not one word was said as we drove back home that dark night.

When we got home, I laid on the air mattress of our apartment's single bedroom. My mom eventually came over and sat next to me on the covers.

"How are you, Sean?" she asked. I was surprised she finally decided to talk to me.

"I'm okay, except my arm and ribs are killing me." I replied, squinting my eyes from the pain.

"Get some rest, okay? I'll give you some ice tomorrow and then we can talk about all this," she said.

I nodded as my mom left the room to sleep on the couch. I tried to go to sleep, but I couldn't. Normally my mother wasn't so nice, but I guessed she was just glad I was alive.

I kept replaying the scene in my head, when I got beaten up by those three Sackers. I remembered the one who yanked me by my hood. His face haunted me, with his beard and menacing dark eyes, thirsty for blood. I had a wretched feeling inside of me, a need for vengeance.

I eventually grew tired, but I was bitter from how the white cops treated me. "Fuck the police!" was my last thought before I drifted asleep.

I woke up the next morning with every part of my body feeling sore.

I was in the middle of my morning routine when my mom saw me getting dressed. "What are you dressin' for, baby?" she asked, peering from the door into the bathroom.

"Um, getting ready for school," I said, confused.

"You ain't goin' to school today, not with them injuries."

"Really?" I asked with astonishment.

"Yeah, I'm not letting my baby go back out there while he's injured!" I hugged my mom with gratitude. It angered me that Tyreek wasn't here to give me a hug, that he was probably hungover at a friend's house. I didn't let it faze me too much, though. After all, I had a whole day off of school.

Later that day, I used ice for my right arm and ribs as I watched television. Earlier my mom said that my arm was probably sprained, but I didn't know how long that would last. Even though I was injured, I still wanted to get payback on those Sacker scumbags.

Before I could continue plotting my revenge, the *Rocky* movie came on the channel. I laid there on the couch, a memory coming to mind.

It was in the Spring of our sixth grade year, Devon and I were walking home after school as I was talking about my film class.

"Yeah, Devon, it was so cool today! We started filmin' a movie that was a spin-off of *Rocky*, and I was leadin' the crew and tellin' 'em everything to do!" I said.

"You watched *Rocky* so many times, no wonder she let you join!" Devon said. We both laughed, Devon was wearing his signature round glasses that he still wore to this day, with a new shirt his dad bought him. (His dad didn't usually buy him much).

I had a fresh cut and Ty's clean black bomber jacket on that I've been begging for him to let me use all week. We both felt confident and that day was one of the best days of our lives, or at least for that moment.

We stopped at the good old Fyre corner store (named after the owner) and went in to get some snacks with the three dollars my mom gave me. Devon got sour worms and I got some chips.

Fyre's store was the go-to food store for most of Sacktown, especially since it was a Black-owned business. It must have been hard for Fyre to run the store though, I didn't exactly know his age but he seemed very old with his ivy cap and old-school glasses. "Some people are feelin' good today!" said Old Man Fyre as he handed us our change.

"Yup!" said Devon with a large grin on his face. We skipped out of the store, both smiling.

We were only one block away from our apartment. Walking down the street on the sidewalk we saw three kids ahead of us.

"Uh-oh, Sean, um, I think we should take another way home," said Devon.

"What? Why? We're only a block away!" I said.

"Well, those are the bullies that I encountered last week, remember? Marty and his crew!"

"Man, my big brother is Tyreek! They can't scare me away!" I exclaimed.

Devon sighed. "Here they come." The three kids grew crooked grins as they stopped in front of us.

"I like that jacket, hand it over," said Marty, the leader.

"N-no!" I stammered. They towered over us and I felt my legs wobble as I stepped back from them.

"Oh really?" said Marty. "Then we'll just have to take it from you!" when he said that the two other kids grabbed me and Marty forced my jacket off. I grunted as they pushed me aside.

"Stop, please! Why are you guys so mean?" said Devon.

"Wait a minute, aren't you that kid that we beat

up last week, you want some more?" exclaimed Marty as he pushed Devon to the ground into a muddy puddle. His new shirt was ruined. Devon whimpered and tried to keep himself from crying.

"Ooh, this jacket is nice!" the bully said as he put on my jacket, the other two just chuckled.

Searing anger coursed through my veins when he put my jacket on. I charged into Marty and head-butted him with my hard skull. Marty stumbled to the ground.

"D-don't just stand there, get him!" said Marty with his hand over his head, the other two pushed me into the brick wall of the apartment beside us.

"What the hell!?" I heard someone say from about a block away. Fast footsteps got louder and louder. I looked to see Tyreek and Ray rushing toward the bullies, and before the bullies realized it they got jumped. Tyreek pounced onto Marty and knocked him out with a quick right, and the other two couldn't evade Ray as he tripped them and stomped them down.

"You okay, Sean?" asked Ty after he took my jacket from Marty.

"Y-yeah," I said. Ty helped me up. "Thanks, big bro," I said as I hugged him.

Later that night in our apartment we could hear Devon getting beat upstairs. We could hear him crying and wailing. He got whooped all night by his drunk father, all because his new shirt got dirty.

I cried for Devon that night. Sacktown was cruel, but that was nothing new.

In the afternoon my mother sat next to me on the couch as I was watching the end of *Rocky*.

"Sean, we have to talk," she said.

I sighed and turned off the television. "What's up?" I said casually, trying to hide my emotions.

"What's happened to you?" she asked.

"Ma, what do you mean?"

"I swear, ever since you've joined that good-for-nothin' gang, you've acted different!"

"The Tyrants aren't changin' who I am, ma! I'm just growing up!"

"Sean, you know that you lyin'! You used to be better than this, now you act like every other hood-lum on the block!"

"Oh yeah, what does that have to do with anything!?"

"You're just not the same, and that's why you've gotten into this mess!"

"Really? That was just because some Sackers came along and jumped me!"

"Would it make you as much of a target if you weren't a gang member?" I grew silent as I looked down. What if she was right? I thought the Tyrants would give me power, but maybe they've just brought me down.

"When I picked up that phone call from the police station, I was in denial. But when I heard your voice, Sean," my mother stopped, I gave her a tissue to wipe her tears away. "I don't want my baby to be put in jail, or even get killed!"

I consoled her with a hug.

"I won't die, ma, I won't die," I said.

The next day my body healed enough for mom to let me go to school with Ray and Ty.

"We gotta get revenge on them sucker Sackers!"

Ty said angrily after I told Ray what happened after the football game, Ty was even angrier hearing it a second time.

"And how are we going to do that?" asked Ray, retwisting his cornrows.

"I know that Jason has some heat on him," said Ty.

"Really, guys, we're gonna kill 'em?" I said, maybe Ty was overreacting. Sure, I hated them, but I didn't want to kill nobody!

"Sean's right, man, we don't even know the guys who jumped him!" said Ray, but that was wrong. I had a rough memory of one of them.

"Yeah, we do," said Ty. "You remember their faces, bro?"

"Nah, it was dark and they were all wearin' hoods." I lied.

"Well, I guess that settles it." said Ray.

"Whatever," Ty said. After what my mom told me, I was reluctant to do any gangbanging.

CHAPTER 3

One week after the incident I didn't feel much more pain from my injuries, except from my right arm. Those guys must have kicked me real hard for me to get this bad of a sprain.

Everyone at Rosewall High heard about what happened to me, and even though I got jumped by three older guys, I still felt crappy about my loss. I didn't like seeming weak, it was one of the reasons I joined the Tyrants, to seem powerful.

During lunch I decided to sit next to Devon in the cafeteria instead of my Tyrant friends. Not only because I was rethinking the gang lifestyle, but also because Devon's been distant ever since he's heard about me getting jumped and arrested.

After I got my food I walked over to Devon's table, but I could already tell something was off. As I was heading over Devon looked around to see if others were watching.

"What's up, Devon?" I said as I sat down next to him. Devon glared at me through his glasses.

"Why are you here?" he grunted.

"I was just checkin' in, I felt like you'd feel lonely since you sit by yourself every day," I said jokingly, but he didn't think it was funny.

"I don't want to be seen with a troublemaker," said Devon.

"Are you talkin' 'bout last week, with me and the cops?" I asked.

"What do you think?"

"Devon, I ain't do nothin'! Some random guys came and beat me up!" I pleaded.

"Were they really random, or are they from your rival gang seeking vengeance for something you did?"

"What do you mean?"

"I mean that ever since you've joined that gang you've never been the same! You became nothing but a hoodlum!"

"I-I—"

Devon cut me off. "I thought you wouldn't fall into the trap of the streets, but last week proved me wrong," Devon said. I was confused, in denial that this was how Devon felt. I was his only friend, the only person who would treat this nerd well, and this was how he repaid me?

"Whatever, punk!" I said as my anger took me over, and walked back to my Tyrant group.

Tyreek and I sat on the porch of Dwayne's house. We were chilling, gazing at the setting sun.

I knew that I'd have to manage drugs with Dwayne sooner or later, but I couldn't stop thinking about what my mom and Devon said.

I thought being in a gang meant full protection, but I was wrong. Now I had my mom worried sick about me and Devon acting like a stranger.

I bit down on my lip, remembering back when we were best friends. I wasn't popular, but no one would bully me because of my big brother Ty. I didn't want to lose Devon. I began to miss my old ways, life before the gang.

Today wasn't Devon and I's first time arguing. Once I became a Tyrant I got popular, and even kids like Marty liked me. I started spending more time with the Tyrants than Devon, and we grew distant.

Devon never looked down on me before though, despite how much of a bad influence I was with an infamous brother and a bad temper. He's been loyal to me ever since we got paired up for that second grade science project. I didn't know why the fact that Devon was so different to me kept us so close. He gave me a sense of hope sometimes, hope that something else was out there for us.

I wanted to put the blame on Devon for our friendship going downhill, for drifting away from me. But the more I thought about it the more I started feeling like Devon was right. Was it too late to apologize?

A loud yell from Tyreek inside interrupted my thoughts, I didn't even realize that Tyreek left me on the porch. I walked inside and saw Tyreek and Dwayne playing a fighting game.

"Damn, Sergeant D! You spammin'!" exclaimed Tyreek.

"Seriously, stop callin' me that. The joke's over,"

said Dwayne. Tyreek chuckled.

"My bad, Sergeant D," he said. I couldn't help but laugh. Dwayne sighed in annoyance.

"Hop on the sticks, Sean," he said.

"A'ight," I said, getting on the couch and grabbing Ty's controller.

As we were playing, I grew curious. "Hey, Dwayne, do you..." I was reluctant to ask.

"Yes?" Dwayne said.

"Do you think gang life is worth it?" I asked. Tyreek and Dwayne looked at me sideways, as if I was crazy to even be asking that.

Dwayne turned off the game and his face grew cold. "Why are you asking that?"

"Uh, it's not like I'm rethinking my life with the Tyrants. I-I'm just asking so I could tell my mom, 'cuz she's worried about how I got arrested and everything," I anxiously lied.

Dwayne lightened up from his cold tone. "Sean, the Tyrants are your family. Tell your ma that it's none of her business, a'ight." I nodded. "You know, Sean, the Tyrant gang is in your blood. Your father used to be a Tyrant."

"Yeah, I know," I said.

"Your dad and my pops, they were the most ruthless of the Tyrants, they ran the gang and got it to where it is now," said Dwayne. "If that's not enough inspiration to be proud of yourself as a Tyrant and tell off your mom, then I don't know what is."

Part of me agreed with Dwayne, but I also felt like I may have been able to make better decisions for my life.

"Anyway, Sean, go ahead and find my charger in my bedroom. It should be there somewhere, look carefully," said Dwayne. I nodded.

"I can help—" Tyreek paused in the middle of his sentence when he saw Dwayne glaring at him. "N-nevermind." The tense energy in the living room made me leave and go to look for Dwayne's charger.

I looked through Dwayne's dresser, under his bed, in his bed, still nothing. Murmuring coming from the living room across the hall traveled to my ears, and I crept to the edge of the doorway to listen.

"You heard that man? After that incident ,Sean is scared to be a fuckin' Tyrant!" Dwayne said quietly.

"Any kid's gonna be scared after somethin' like that man! He's only fourteen, give him a break," Ty whispered.

"Nah, I gotta test his allegiance to the gang. He's too doubtful, if he stays scared like that again he might do somethin' stupid, like snitchin'."

"My brother would never do dat! My brother grew up with the gang man, don't say no stupid shit like dat!" said Ty, trying to keep quiet with his loud emotions.

"You never know, so I gotta test him. Soon I'ma see if he'll…" Dwayne stopped talking as he looked across the hallway. I quickly shifted away from the doorway, escaping his line of sight. After that I kept searching for the charger, not risking getting caught by listening to their conversation.

Five more minutes passed and I still couldn't find it, at this point I just assumed it was a lie to let Dwayne talk to Tyreek. I made my way back to the living room.

"Couldn't find it?" said Dwayne. I nodded.

"A'ight, I think it's time that we head home anyway," said Tyreek. Dwayne agreed and we left his house.

We were a few blocks away from our apartment when Ty and I started getting hungry. "Damn, I'm lowkey tired of walkin' out here! Like, think about it. Every day we walk to school, and about once or twice a week we walk to Dwayne's. Now that's a lot of miles!" said Ty. I laughed.

"You're a junior. You're old enough to drive now, why don't you?" I asked.

"I failed my driving test, remember?" said Tyreek. I laughed even harder, I only brought that up so he would mention it again. Tyreek sighed. "CJ's bum ass never wants to pick me up either."

"His blue mustang's cheap anyway!" I said, we both busted out laughing until we stopped at the Fyre corner store. We walked in and got a few snacks.

As Tyreek was looking for a tuna sandwich I could see a faint red mark on his face. Where was that from? I shook it off not wanting to get too deep in my thoughts again. "Yo, Ty, have you seen dad run the streets like Dwayne saw?" I said to get my mind on something else.

Ty chuckled, "Haha, nah. I was a baby then, and when I grew up dad left."

"Your father really was something though," said Old Man Fyre. "He ran these streets back in the day like it was a track field! Yeah, the Harper brothers, them two was somethin' else!"

"Can you tell us more?" I asked.

Fyre tipped his oval glasses. "I don't know how your mother would feel about that. Y'all should be gettin' home now anyways, it's dark out," he replied. We paid for our food and left.

The dark night reminded me of what had happened a week ago. I wish Tyreek would have protected me then, but I wasn't going to cry and whine about it. I didn't have to rely on Ty for everything, but I was glad I finally got to spend some time with my brother. We haven't done that lately.

Our mom was asleep on the couch, probably exhausted from work. Ty and I went to the single bedroom and watched movies until we fell asleep on our shared air mattress.

The next day I walked to Rosewall High with Ray and

Ty.

"Yo, Ty, the gang's gonna be bettin' on a car race after dealin' today, you down?" asked Ray. Of course, he didn't ask me.

"Yeah, man, I'm down!" Ty said. "Sean, you comin'?" I remembered the job with Dwayne I had later today.

"Nah, I'm good," I said.

Soon enough, the job came along. After school I walked over to Dwayne's house, with each step I could hear my skippy heart beating more and more rapidly. I knocked on the door and Dwayne opened it quickly.

"'Sup," I said nervously.

"A'ight, let's go," he said. As he walked over to his beat-up car, I looked closer to see bullet holes in the sides of it.

"Wait, where are we going?"

"Let's get straight to business, we're going to a Latino's house," he replied.

"What, why?"

"You'll see," he said as he motioned me to get in

the car. I sat in the passenger seat and braced myself for what we were about to do.

Throughout the whole car ride we didn't talk. I thought we'd make some conversation since the ride was over forty minutes, but that wasn't the case.

Starting conversation with Tyreek wasn't hard at all. I was never able to spend too much time with Tyreek since he joined the Tyrants, and me becoming a Tyrant myself hadn't changed that. I'd probably be able to chill with him again soon, hopefully.

We finally arrived at our destination. I supposed that we were about to enter a stash house, but the light brown house we were in front of wasn't like the ones in the movies. The house was only two stories high and inside there was Dominican bachata playing. Dwayne did a secret knock on the door.

"Remember that pattern." said Dwayne. I nodded as a Hispanic guy answered the door.

"Sup, Sergeant D?" the man said.

"You already know why I'm here, man," said Dwayne.

"Alright, alright," he said. The man then looked at me. "Ayo, who is this?"

"Don't worry 'bout him, he's like my secretary," Dwayne said.

"Yeah, all right. Come in." the guy said. He was pretty short, especially compared to the big bodyguards inside.

Dwayne and I sat on an old-fashioned couch facing who seemed like the leader. He had some hair, unlike his bodyguards next to him. The leader was sitting with his cigar still in his mouth.

"Let's get straight to business, Marco. Y'all been runnin' smooth with dem imports right?" asked Dwayne. The leader took the cigar out of his mouth.

"The imports from the DR have gone well, no interruptions," said Marco, the leader. He was more fluent in English than his henchmen.

"Okay, you got the stash?" asked Dwayne.

"Yeah," Marco said, he then said something in Spanish to one of his bodyguards and they pulled out a suitcase. I found it weird how only the leader was wearing a suit and tie while the others had tank tops on.

"A'ight, Marco, here's your cash," Dwayne said as he pulled out what must have been $2,000 out of his pocket and gave it to Marco.

"Carry the bag," Dwayne said assertively, I followed his orders without hesitation.

"Nice doin' business, Sergeant D," Marco said as we left. Dwayne nodded.

The reality slowly came back to me after we left the house that I actually participated in a drug deal! This whole thing was illegal! It wasn't like fighting or stealing, this was the type of stuff the FBI covered!

"So, what now?" I asked as we were driving away.

"Today, Sean, we rest. You did good," replied Dwayne. His compliment went through one ear and out the other as I was contemplating the legality of this whole deal; my conscience was questioning this lifestyle even more now.

"Yo, I don't want another run-in with the cops man, it's too—" I got cut off.

"Shut up, Sean, it's all business! You just don't understand. Sit back and learn, that's why I brought you here!" he exclaimed. We stayed quiet for the rest of the ride as he drove me home to my apartment. We didn't even say goodbye.

With business, Dwayne wasn't Dwayne. He was a whole different person, and Sergeant D was his name.

CHAPTER 4

I was resting on the air mattress of our apartment's bedroom when I heard a car beeping. I looked out of my apartment window to see CJ and Ray waiting for us to hop in.

After I quickly got dressed my mom busted into the room.

"Boy, what are you doin' gettin' dressed like this?" she asked.

"Oh, I'm just goin' out with some friends, ma," I said.

"Hmm," she said, looking me up and down as if I was suspicious.

Ty, who was already dressed, came into the room. "Come on, Sean, let's go!" he said, excited. Tyreek then pulled me away.

"Bye, ma!" I said as I rushed out of the apartment. There was no better time to hang with the guys than Saturday. Tyreek and I got into the backseat of CJ's blue Mustang as Ray put on some hip-hop.

"What's goin' on, fam?" Tyreek said.

"What's good, Ty, Sean?" Ray said with a dark emphasis on my name.

"What took y'all so long, man?" asked CJ.

"Man, Sean almost got busted by our mom!" Ty said.

"Damn, man, I don't want my nice new car waitin' out here to get jacked up!" CJ said as he drove away. "You don't know what these Sackers might do!"

"Tell me about it," I said.

"You know what, we never got revenge on them Sacker Suckers!" said Ty. Despite what my mother told me, revenge was still a recurring theme in my mind, especially since my sprain had finally healed.

"Yeah, I'd like that!" said Ray.

"What, you gon' show them your new boxing moves you whipped up after your loss in the summer?" CJ said, chuckling.

"Probably, if they want the smoke!" Ray said as he looked at me. I stared back at him, and Tyreek must have noticed because he told CJ to turn the music up. I got a bad vibe from Ray, and I could tell nothing good could come from our tension.

CJ parked the car around Rosewall Park. "Come on y'all, let's get some cash before we get somethin' to eat," he said. We all got out of the Mustang ready for action.

We walked around the grassy park, looking for someone, anyone who had some money. It would be better to do this in the dark, but we were all too impatient to wait that long for some food.

Stealing didn't represent gangbanging for me, the white man stole from us enough. Besides, I wasn't a punk.

Eventually we found our victim, a guy with a silver chain and a nice polo shirt who looked like he had some good cash. I looked around, no one was anywhere near us. The four of us crept up behind the man on the sidewalk, and before he could suspect us it was too late.

CJ rushed ahead and put the man in a headlock, the man screamed for a bit but CJ covered the man's mouth and said through his teeth, "Shut the fuck up!"

Tyreek grinned, saying, "Yeah, give us your money! All of it!"

The wide-eyed man tried to yell but couldn't; CJ's headlock was real tight. At this point all of us were circled around the guy and were ready to get to business.

"You think I'm playin', man!?" Tyreek exclaimed, he then punched the man in the stomach.

"Stop screamin', bitch!" said Ray, punching the guy in his face. I just stood there, starting to feel uneasy as I kept watch.

The man's murmuring stopped and he calmed down, not wanting to get punched again. Tyreek searched through the guy's pockets and took his wallet from him. Ty took all the cash from it and then threw the wallet away.

CJ threw the man to the ground and we all kicked and stomped the man. He screamed and wailed and cried, but we all just kept kicking him, I even stomped his face a few times. We did that for about a minute until the guy grew quiet. Was he dead? Was this murder? I started walking back from the man, fear in my eyes.

"Don't worry," Ty said. "He's only unconscious, now let's get outta here!". We all ran back to CJ's car and made our way to the Streamville cafe.

After driving, bragging about the cash we stole from the guy, and listening to cool hip-hop, we got to the cafe. When I first became a Tyrant, I went out and did stuff like this with the gang all the time, but never have I seen such a violent mugging to this degree. The man's face haunted me, battered, swollen, and beaten, his tan skin covered in red. It did get some anger off my chest for the Sackers, but I wondered if I was only able to do this because I had others with me.

I shook my thoughts off as we got inside the empty cafe and ordered some food with a lot of fries. The white cashier looked at us funny, as if we were going to rob him. We should have robbed him because of how he looked at us.

"Racist punks, we should've just gone to the Fyre corner store," CJ said as he chowed down on his hamburger. "Can't even enjoy a sandwich out here!"

I felt a weight on my chest and started to feel guilty about the mugging we did, as if that was why we deserved to be glared at by the white cashier.

"Yeah, those wretched white cops arrested Sean for no reason!" Ty said, eating his fries. "And when they couldn't find anything he did wrong they just let him go like nothing happened!"

"This is some bullshit!" CJ said, hammering the table with his fist. The cashier gave us an odd stare but we ignored it and continued eating.

"I'ma go to the bathroom," my brother said as he finished up his food.

"Really, that dirty-ass public restroom?" said Ray, chuckling.

"Yeah, yeah, whatever!" Ty said as he went to the bathroom.

"Man, I'm pissed!" said CJ.

"Yeah, I can't wait to get revenge on them Sackers!" I said.

"Really, Sean? You've never even held a gun before, are you sure you're ready for payback?" Ray said.

"What?" I said with disbelief.

"I feel like you're too much of a bitch to get payback, especially since you pleaded to Devon, the little

49

nerd, to be your friend," Ray said.

My fists balled up. "Don't talk about Devon like that!" I said as I got up from the tables. Ray stood and we stared each other down.

"Well, what'chu gonna do about it, punk?" Ray asked, getting up in my face. My veins almost popped as Ray got on my last nerve by pushing me away.

I swung at him, but he easily ducked and landed a blow to my stomach. I stumbled back, shocked. Ray was a boxer, so what did I expect?

I got back into the fight, this time blocking and being more cautious. That didn't matter though, because Ray threw a straight punch to my face. It was so fast and so strong that I couldn't block it.

My head flew back from the impact. This wasn't like our fight in the summer at all! This was real, no gloves and no games. I looked at CJ, he was just watching us, enjoying his drink.

I shook my head to get back into it. Ray dashed toward me and threw another punch, but somehow I dodged it and forcefully tripped him. Ray fell face-first to the ground right as Ty got out of the bathroom.

"What the hell!?" Ty said as he saw us. Ray got up and grabbed me by my shirt. I saw his face, so angry and filled with hatred that my heart dropped. "Woah, stop!" Ty said, breaking up the fight. "What in the hell happened?"

I was speechless.

"We were rumblin'," Ray said.

"What!? Why?" Ty asked.

"Man, ever since the summer I hated this nigga! I trained all my damn life in boxing just to get beaten by this weak kid?" Ray said.

"It was just a trial, Ray!" Tyreek exclaimed.

"And this was just a fight!" Ray countered.

Tyreek shook his head and looked at CJ. "Why didn't you do nothin', man?" he asked.

"Shit, they was rumblin'? That's their business." CJ said.

"Y'all are whack, man!" Ty said.

"Come on, CJ, let's go." Ray said. And just like that it was over. Ray and CJ drove off in the Mustang.

Tyreek looked at me. "Damnit, Sean, you got a

bloody nose, man." I wiped my nose with my index finger and saw the blood. Tyreek looked at the cashier; he seemed shocked but quickly looked away.

Tyreek grabbed some tissues for my nose and we left. Walking home was long, but it was better than if we drove with Ray. At least the sun was setting and the view was nice

"Man, why'd Ray do that!?" said Tyreek angrily on our way home.

"He hates me and I hate him, that's why!" I said, tissues still in my nose.

"Yeah, but … we was best friends, ride or die! I shoulda known somethin' like dis'd happen!" he said.

"What? Why?" I asked.

"You don't think I noticed the shade Ray was throwin' at you since the summer, even on our walks to school he'd be hostile! I wish y'all coulda just been cool, but instead all dis shit happened!" I could tell Ty really cared about Ray, they were almost like me and Devon.

I wondered why I got mad and fought Ray to defend Devon. Did I still consider Devon a friend after he stereotyped me as every other Sacktown Tyrant? I just didn't know.

"Ty?"

"Yeah?"

"What do you want to be in life?"

"C'mon Sean, you know what I wanna be, a track star!"

"How are you gonna do dat by smokin' all the time? You know it ain't good for you, especially if you wanna do track!"

Ty sighed. "Did mom ask you to talk to me 'bout dis?"

"No, she didn't. You always say 'Tyrant gang for life!' but the Tyrants ain't gonna get you outta here, they just gonna drag you down, Ty!"

"The Tyrants been there for me my whole life! They been there for you too! They ain't gonna bring me down!" Ty exclaimed.

I sighed as my anger subsided into sorrow. I just wanted better for my brother, I was tired of Sacktown! It was like we could never get out of these projects, maybe this was just how it was meant to be. My brother patted me on the back when he noticed I was getting emotional.

"It's a'ight Sean. Sacktown's a cruel place, but we'll survive. We just gotta keep workin' to feed ma and keep a roof up over our heads, get outta these projects." I looked at Ty, I wondered how he always stayed so positive, how he made light of every situation.

There was nobody else around that afternoon but I still felt embarrassed for my tears. Tyreek and I hugged, and I wished that hug would last forever.

CHAPTER 5

At Dwayne's house, him and I were getting ready to go out and check in on all of the Tyrant dealers. The Tyrants were spread out through most of Sacktown, beside Sacker territory.

Dwayne and I drove off. This was my second time checking in on our dealers with Dwayne, or Sergeant D. I've learned that the Dwayne I know is absent when he's doing business, and he's replaced by the cruel entity of Sergeant D.

"So, I heard you and Ray got some beef," said Dwayne.

"Yeah, I threw hands with him at the Stream-ville cafe yesterday," I replied. Dwayne huffed harshly through his nose and looked in the rearview mirror of the car, trying to hold back his anger. "What's wrong?" I asked.

"Damnit, Sean!" Dwayne said loudly through gritted teeth.

"What?" I asked. "Ray was the one who started the fight."

"As a leader you can't have beef with other Tyrants!" he exclaimed as he made a turn into Rosewall Park. How could he be so mad over a fight?

"What do you mean by leader? I never signed up for this!" I said.

"Well, you had to pull your weight sooner or later!" Dwayne said as he parked near some of our dealers in Rosewall Park.

"Yeah, I know but… can't I just do what Tyreek does, deal drugs and chill?" I asked.

"Do you always want to follow in Tyreek's footsteps? Do you want to live in his shadow?" Dwayne said. I grunted; he was right. After all, Tyreek wasn't the only reason I became a Tyrant. It was for the power! I didn't want to be unpopular, I didn't want to be weak, and I didn't want to see my mom struggling anymore.

I sighed, "No, I'm my own man but—"

"Then act like it!" Dwayne interrupted. "You should want to be better than your brother, not a clone of 'em." I looked down, feeling a bit shamed by my big cousin. "Come on, let's go," Dwayne said as he got out of the car.

We walked over to some fellow Tyrants who just finished business with a really old guy who looked like he shouldn't be using drugs.

"'Sup, Sergeant D?" said CJ. He was with the dealers at the park, chilling and getting work done.

"You already know what time it is, how's business?" asked Dwayne with no emotion.

"We got seven hunnit, it was a pretty lazy day," CJ answered as he handed Dwayne the money. Dwayne counted it and gave CJ and the two Tyrants with him each $150. "'Preciate it, Sergeant D," said CJ.

"A'ight, y'all done for the day. Enjoy y'all Sunday," said Dwayne. We then went back into the car and repeated the process. We met other Tyrants near Rosewall High and then at a corner near Fyre's store not many blocks away from my apartment. Luckily, I didn't see Ray, but I didn't see Tyreek either. Usually, Tyreek dealt at that corner with Ray, but neither of them were there.

When Dwayne and I finished checking in with all the Tyrant dealers Dwyane had the same question as me. "You know where Tyreek's at?" he asked.

"Nah, I'm as confused as you," I said.

"A'ight, well, here you go." said Dwayne as he handed me $50. I stared at the money.

"Th-thanks, Dwayne, I mean, Sergeant D!" I said as I took the cash.

"Don't worry 'bout it, enjoy your Sunday, man," he said. I nodded and walked home since we finished our work at the corner just a few blocks away from my apartment.

As soon as I got home I knew what time it was. My mom had a nice dress on with a Bible in her hand. She had her gospel music playing and she was clapping to the beat.

"Sean?" my mom said as she turned off the music.

"Hi, ma," I said.

"And where were you at while I was waitin' here for my babies?" she asked.

I sighed. "Sorry ma," I apologized.

"You know where Tyreek's at?" she asked.

"No, he's not here?"

"Well, I guess he gon' be late for church again." My mom seemed sad. She was so passionate about church, Tyreek says that she's been that way ever since dad's been incarcerated. She never even bothered to tell me what he was locked up for. "Anyway, get ready for church before we run late!" my mom said.

I headed to the bedroom and looked through the closet for my hand-me-down suit. Next to the closet I saw an old hole in the wall from when I punched through it 2 years ago. It was June 18, 2000, Father's Day. I didn't even know what that deadbeat looked like.

When I got ready, we went to church. I was never so enthusiastic about it, I only ever went there because my mom liked it. When we got to church I could see Devon there with his aunts; his father never went to church. I looked at him, but he acted like he didn't notice me. I even saw Ray once the choir sang the songs and everyone got up to rejoice and sing; I didn't pay him any mind though.

I looked around for Tyreek our whole time at church, but he never came. I wondered how mom was going to scold him tonight. Tyreek was probably out smoking weed at CJ's. They always got the weed from Marco and his guys; had it been anyone else Dwayne would have been pissed.

After church mom and I went home and waited. Eight hours passed and Tyreek still wasn't home. It was 11:00 PM at this point and I was mad. I could hear my mom crying in the bedroom as I was on the couch.

This all wasn't new with Ty, but I was tired of him always doing drugs with other Tyrants and leaving mom and I here to rot! He didn't even care to show up to church, knowing how much mom cared about it!

I couldn't take it anymore, after my incident with the cops and the Sackers I've seen how painful it was for my mom to watch us being involved with gangs. Sure, I was still hanging out with the Tyrants and helping Dwayne with dealing drugs, but I was doing it to support mom, and I assured myself that I wouldn't worry her anymore. But Tyreek was always slacking off and doing weed!

I got dressed and walked over to my mom in our apartment's single bedroom. I saw her blowing her nose as she cried. I balled up my fists. "I'ma go look for Tyreek," I said.

"No, please! I don't want two of my sons gone!" she said, continuing to cry.

I hugged my mom and comforted her. "I know where he is, I'll be back soon." I reassured her.

She looked at me with sincere sorrow. "Okay," she said. "I love you, Sean."

"I love you too," I said with a dark voice.

The first place I looked was at CJ's house. It was only a few blocks away from my apartment, and CJ was always down to smoke weed.

The harsh sound of rain hitting the ground filled the silent night. I kept my guard up as I started to walk faster, looking out for any Sackers. I soon arrived and knocked on CJ's door, but his mother answered it.

"What you doin' over here, child?" she asked.

"I'm looking for my brother Tyreek, is he here with CJ?" I asked.

"CJ's downstairs with some friends, you can go and see if your brother's there with 'em," she said.

I thanked her and walked into the basement. When I did, all I saw was CJ, Ray, and two other high Tyrants chilling on a couch. I looked at Ray with resentment, but quickly turned my focus to CJ.

"CJ, it's Sean," I said. They all looked so high I didn't know if they could tell it was me.

"Ohh, wassup, Sean?" said CJ.

"Look I'm in a hurry, did Ty come over here?" I asked.

"Nahhh mannn, he wasn't here," CJ said. I never saw anyone this high before.

"A'ight, thanks. I'ma head out now," I said as I walked away.

"Wait, Sean," CJ said, I looked back at him. "You don't wanna chill and," CJ smoked another ring, "chill and smoke man?"

"Nah, I'm good. I'ma see y'all tomorrow though, peace!" I said. If Tyreek wasn't chilling and smoking, then he must have been at Dwayne's house.

I hurried using a shortcut that I knew, it was close to Sacker territory but I didn't want to worry my mom for long. I dashed from alley to alley, my frustration with Tyreek sustaining my energy.

If he had been with me after the football game, I wouldn't have gotten jumped. If he didn't smoke all the time, maybe mom wouldn't always be so worried about him. If he focused on track more, maybe he could have been a better role model to me! If he paid more attention to me, if he spent more time with me, if he loved me...

I was almost at Dwayne's house when I smelled something strong up ahead. I went and turned into an alley to check it out, but I almost passed out when I saw it.

I went back home and into the bedroom.

"Well, where's Tyreek?" she asked, she seemed less emotional now.

"There was a dead body in an alley," I said.

"Oh my God, who was it? Hopefully the police find the body, but we shouldn't say anything, okay, Sean? You can't get in trouble with the police again, okay, but—" she rambled, but I cut her off.

"Ma, it was Tyreek."

CHAPTER 6

Walking to school alone was nothing to me now. It's been over a week since Tyreek's death, but it only started getting to me at that point.

At school my ideas were clouded with anger, and I couldn't get my mind off the image of Tyreek's dead body.

"Sean, can you solve the problem that's on the board?" said my math teacher.

I looked up at the board from my crossed arms to solve the problem. However, when I saw random numbers that I couldn't focus on, I just said, "I can't solve it," and put my head back down in my arms.

"Excuse me?" said my teacher. "We've been going over these types of equations for the whole unit! Have you been studying, Sean?"

Was she serious? The only person who studied

in this class was Devon! "It doesn't matter, math is useless anyway!" I exclaimed. My teacher just stood there, shocked, until she told me to wait outside of the classroom.

I went out and sat by the classroom door. I knew I was acting childish but I didn't know how to feel. Word about Tyreek's death spread around Rosewall High quickly, and every day at lunch the Tyrants talked about it and asked me questions. It just made me so... mad!

I banged the cement wall behind me so hard I felt like everyone in class could hear it, but I didn't care. I couldn't care less about anyone but my family, the people who wouldn't ignore my brother's death like my math teacher probably did.

My teacher came out from the classroom. "Stand up," she said. I stood up and I was almost as tall as her. My caucasian teacher knew I was a Tyrant, and she paused when she saw my balled-up fists.

"Well, uh, just try to study more, okay? I don't want you to fall behind," she said with a changed attitude. She let me back in the class and I noticed Devon staring at me. What did he want?

Later that day I went to Dwayne's house. I was

expecting to check in with Marco and get our drugs, but surprisingly Jason was there. Jason glared at me with those hard eyes of his; small things like that reminded me of his reputation as an assassin.

When Dwayne let me in, Jason and him nodded to each other. Then Jason said, "Sean, Sergeant D and I have been talkin', and there's someone who hasn't paid what they owed."

"What? How? Don't they gotta pay before they get the drugs?" I asked.

"Yeah, but this guy was a trusted customer," Jason said. "He said that he'd definitely get the money to pay us back, at least accordin' to CJ."

"So, CJ let this guy go with the drugs?" I asked.

"You know that idiot," Dwayne said. "Anyway, I want you to go with Jason to take care of that guy."

"What? Jason's pretty much an assassin, I don't got no experience with dis!"

"Sean, as a Tyrant you gotta build up your rep. You can't trust anyone who doesn't respect you as their leader!" said Dwayne. I sighed.

"A'ight, I'll do it," I said. I didn't want to get in

trouble with the police again, but if nobody knew then there wouldn't be a problem.

"That's what I'm talkin' 'bout, roll out with Jason and get dis punk!" said Dwayne. I nodded and went with Jason in his car.

During the car ride Jason and I didn't talk. I knew Jason was the silent type so I didn't bother to start any conversation. Jason was a cold-blooded killer, and in the car I was thinking if I'd be like him that night.

Before I knew it, we arrived at the guy's house. Jason looked at me and we nodded to each other. We put on black cloth masks over our faces, Jason then reached into the glove compartment and gave me what looked like a Glock. It was heavier than I thought it would be.

I looked at him, and then at the gun, contemplating that a lethal weapon was in my hand.

"It's loaded, so be careful." Jason said.

"B-but I don't know how to use a gun and—" I stammered.

"Shut up, it's business. You better learn how to use it today, because the guy we're tryna kill might try somethin'!" Jason exclaimed in a deep voice, cutting me off.

The cold and slick grip of the heavy pistol made my hands shake. "S-so, that guy can have a gun too?"

"We don't know, that's why we gotta be ready. Enough talkin', let's go." Jason said as he got out of the car. I followed him to the doorstep of the house and we knocked on the door.

After a minute or two a little kid opened the door. Jason just walked past him to look for the man. I looked at the kid, hiding my gun behind my back.

"Where's your daddy?" I asked. He ran upstairs yelling "Daddy, daddy!" I tried to follow him, but I saw Jason talking to a woman in the kitchen of the house. She must have been the little kid's mom because she looked at the running kid with fear.

"Look at me when I'm talkin' to you!" Jason yelled as he pistol-whipped her. I was surprised she wasn't knocked out from that, but Jason pistol-whipped her again and she fell to the floor.

"I'ma check the basement!" Jason said. He was so

different with business, so aggressive. He wasn't the hushed Jason I knew, I guessed this was the true wrath of the Tyrants' assassin. I just nodded at him and went upstairs to the room that the kid went to.

I was shaking in fear; I was actually supposed to kill someone? I pulled my gun out from behind my back, my sweaty hands making the pistol's grip moist. My heart was racing as I made a turn into the open room. I saw a man sitting on a bed. He looked at me so solemnly as if he'd accepted death.

"So, y'all came for the money? Sorry, but I don't got none, not for you Tyrant scum!" he said.

"What'chu mean!?" I asked as I pointed my gun at him, but my hands were so shaky that it seemed impossible to aim.

"What are you gonna do, shoot me? You already ruined my family with them drugs y'all sold me. I can't even be a good father, let alone get enough money to pay you!" he exclaimed as he stood up from his bed. "You Tyrant scum! I hate every last one of y'all! All of you should die!"

At that I could feel the anger coursing through my veins. I remembered Tyreek and everything he did for the Tyrants. I remembered his goofy smile and his warm hugs. The Tyrants have been in my life forever, all of them didn't deserve to die; *Tyreek* didn't deserve to die. Before I knew it my anger took control, and I shot him with no remorse.

The man fell to the floor with a big thud. The kid from earlier came out from a closet next to the bed. He stared down at his dad, shocked. It was as if he was paralyzed. Another dad absent in a home. The job was done.

Later that day I was walking home from Dwayne's house after he gave me some money, a reward for what I did, though nothing could pay off what I just went through. I saw Devon down the block and he ran up to me. I sighed.

"What do you want?" I asked.

"Look, Sean," Devon said as he was gasping for air. "I was wrong to avoid you. I heard that you got arrested for something you didn't do, and I heard about your brother." There was a short pause where we didn't look at each other. Devon continued. "I'm sorry, but I know you, Sean. I know that you're not a ruthless gangster. You don't have to get revenge for your brother, you don't have to kill anyone!"

"You idiot," I said blandly as I was looking down.

"Huh?" Devon said.

I looked up at him and gave him the coldest stare I've ever given in my life. "I already did."

CHAPTER 7

It's been two days since I've had blood on my hands. I never boasted about it or told anyone what I did, besides Devon.

The past two nights I've tried to go to sleep, but too many things have been haunting me. I still wasn't comfortable with having more space on the air mattress to sleep, and with no brother to talk to at night my mind grew even deeper into its thoughts when it was supposed to rest.

Sitting on the couch watching the news alone, I heard a reporter say, "Welcome to Channel 64 News where we inform you all about what's going on in Toussaint County! Today, January 21st, a report surfaced about a man shot to death in his own bedroom. The man had a wife and son who didn't want to comment on anything publicly about the incident. However, harsh bruises were identified on the wife's face! If you know anything more about this incident, call the police immediately and inform them of what you may know!" I switched the television off, tensely gripping the cushion of the couch.

Police sirens whirred by and I tried to control my breathing as I heard the cars drive past the apartment. I tried to convince myself that everything was fine, that no one knew what happened. I stressed over what could happen, but the more outcomes I pondered over the more stressed I became.

I tried to relax and think of a nice memory...

"Hey, Sean," Devon said as we were lolling on two rusty swings in Rosewall Park, gazing at the sunset.

"Yeah?" I said, kicking the chipwood under our feet.

"Do you think there's a better place for us, somewhere outside of this stupid town?" Devon asked. I looked at him, his round glasses gleaming from the sunlight. I looked back at the beautiful sunset.

"What do you mean?" I asked.

"I mean that Sacktown is a place full of drugs and bad people. There has to be a better place out there that has better schools, better influences, better people!"

"I'm sure there's a place like that… but we're not meant for it," I said solemnly, continuing to kick the chipwood.

"What?"

"The white people in other towns and cities don't want us there, they hate us. Why do you think there's barely any white people here in Sacktown?" My voice grew louder with hatred. I roughly kicked the chipwood one last time, showing my frustration. Devon paused, seeing the dark patch of ground uncovered by my onslaughts on the chipwood. We both looked at the sunset.

"That may be true… but I'm gonna prove them wrong! I'm gonna get out of this place!" said Devon. I could tell he was inspired so I didn't say anything else. That left a long pause until Devon changed the subject and talked about our fifth grade math test on fractions. He was always such a nerd, and I somewhat missed that.

The day of Tyreek's funeral came. There hasn't been a moment that's gone by that I haven't thought of him, and I was sure that it was the same for my mother too.

"Sean, are you ready?" my mom asked.

"Yes, ma," I said as I came out of my room. We were both dressed in black, and I could see my mother's tears. I attempted to be her refuge as I consoled and hugged her, but on the inside I felt the exact same way.

After some time, she let go of me and looked me straight in the eyes. "Sean, I don't want you turning out like your cousin, or your father, or even your..." she couldn't even mention Tyreek without breaking down.

"Okay, ma," I grew angry at myself for what happened. Maybe if I'd never joined the Tyrants Tyreek would have never died, or maybe if I just stayed with him that day. Maybe.

At the funeral everything felt so dark, even with the sunlight shining through the colored window panes of the church windows. Slow gospel music played as more and more people entered the church, everyone in black. A lot of Tyrants were there, including CJ and Ray. Devon wasn't there, but at this point I wasn't surprised.

Before I knew it, the music was over and everyone was ready. The reverend was at the podium behind the open casket.

"Hello, everyone, we have come together this day to pay our respects to Tyreek Harper. So, I shall call up people from least closest to closest of family and friends, as his mother informed me to," said the reverend. He then called people up one by one to visit the casket, friends and distant family.

All I could think about was my brother's goofy smile, his crazy energy, our carefree walks through Sacktown, and all my other unique memories of him. To think that I hated him for always going out with friends, he probably knew that one day he was going to die. Whether it was from the police or gangbanging or starvation, he knew he'd die. Maybe that was why he was always full of energy, to live life to its fullest.

"Dwayne Harper may now visit the body," said the reverend. I looked up and saw Dwayne walk over and stare down at Tyreek's dead body. For a second, I thought he shedded some tears, but that was impossible.

"Tyreek Harper's immediate family may now

visit the body," said the reverend.

My mom and I walked up to the body. When we saw Ty's corpse it was almost surreal. My mom was crying and wailing, screaming, "My baby, my baby!" I just stood there as my eyes set up as a perch for a salty waterfall. He was actually dead, no goofy smile, no nothing.

The next day at Dwayne's house, him and I were chilling on his porch. "Yo, do you and Ray still have beef?" asked Dwayne.

I shook my head, "Nah, we talked after the funeral when my mom was talking with family. He apologized and said his condolences for my family and I."

Dwayne nodded. "Yesterday reminded me of somethin'," he said.

"What?"

"Your father and my pops. How they ran the streets, how ruthless the Tyrants were. Two sly criminals, they could have both been rich!"

"So why didn't they? What happened?"

"Your dad got too greedy, he wanted all the power

and fame, he wanted to be the only leader of the Tyrants. So, he killed his brother... my pops." I was surprised when he said that. How come I never knew about this? I felt like crying for Dwayne, but it didn't seem to faze him as his emotionless eyes gazed at the clouds. "Your pops raised me though, so I guess he loved his brother enough to not let me be out there alone."

"Was that why my dad got incarcerated?" I asked. Dwayne stayed quiet. After that there was a long pause, until I thought about my brother again. "Do you think if I was a better brother, Tyreek wouldn't be dead?" I asked.

"It's not your fault Sean... it's mine." Dwayne sighed. "It's my fault."

"But—"

"Just shut up, a'ight!" exclaimed Dwayne. It was quiet again, until suddenly Dwayne's phone was ringing. "Yo, what the fuck?" he said as he picked up the phone. "Yo, what the fuck you callin' me for, CJ? You know I'm with Sean... What?... Marco?... Fuck! A'ight, I'ma hit his crib up." Dwayne stood up and put his phone back in his pocket. "Come on, let's go."

CHAPTER 8

Dwayne's car tires screeched as we made a hard left turn on our way to Marco's. I clutched my seatbelt as Dwayne continued to speed up, thinking of what we were about to do.

Dwayne told me that CJ saw some Sackers with Marco talking about their drug deals somewhere in Sacker territory. That must have been something Marco and his Latino crew weren't supposed to do because now we were headed straight for their necks, the only thing was that I didn't know our exact plan. There must have been about twenty bodyguards with Marco, judging off the times Dwayne and I came here to pick up drugs. What could the two of us do against all of them?

"We gon' burn dat shitty brown house down," said Dwayne as we parked a few blocks down from Marco's miniature stash house.

"How would we do that?" I asked. "Won't we get caught?"

"It's Saturday, Marco's cartel always focuses on imports on the weekends. They won't be guarding the house much. I know this sounds like some shit from a spy movie, but I'ma need you to sneak around to the back of the house and burn it down with dis," Dwayne said as he pulled out a match and lighter from his pocket.

"Really, burn it down with that?" I asked.

"Yeah, there's gasoline in my trunk. That should do some damage, when you finish, run back here."

"A'ight, I'll go," I said. I grabbed the match and the lighter from him and hopped out of the car. Dwayne popped the trunk for me, but I hesitated to take the gasoline. What would Marco's cartel do to us, to me, after this?

"Let's go," Dwayne said. I had no more time to think, I shut off all the circling questions in my head, letting my instinct take over. I walked down the sidewalk with the gasoline as Dwayne stayed in the car. After looking out for anyone watching, I reluctantly hopped a metal fence into Marco's backyard.

My heart was pounding heavily as my crouching footsteps crunched in the grass. As I walked, I poured gasoline all over the house until I got to the back when my inexperience with lighters triggered a fear in my mind. I clicked the lighter on and slowly put the match over it.

I was startled by the instant lighting of the match! I turned the lighter off and looked at the brown house. My hands were shaking as I thought of the deep consequences of being an arsonist and a murderer, the subtle warmth of the match making my worried face glow. I took a deep breath and tossed the match, instantly spreading a fire throughout the house!

I was in awe of how big and fast the fire spread, but then quickly hopped the back fence of the house and ran away without a second thought, forgetting about Dwayne. I didn't look back once. I had no sense of where I was going, but escaping was the only thing on my mind.

In the end Dwayne found me blocks away from the stash house, panting. He picked me up with his car and dropped me off at home. We didn't talk throughout the whole car ride. I expected some sort of reward for what I did, but Dwayne didn't give me anything. Dwayne's aura was off, and I could sense that he was deep in his thoughts.

When I arrived home my mom was watching the news on the couch.

"Hey, ma," I said, closing the door behind me.

"Sean, come over here and sit next to me," my mom said. I knew I was in trouble, but when I sat down on the couch and saw a light brown house in flames on the television, I understood why.

"M-ma, it's not what it looks like," I said, but my sweat gave everything away.

"It's weird because you left with Dwayne and came back here a bit after this event came on the news." she found me out. The fast coverage of the arson on the news surprised me as I tried to think of something to say.

"Ma, I—"

"Sean," she said, cutting me off, "I won't tell nobody. I just want you to stay away from your cousin."

"Dwayne?"

"Yes, he's bad news. I don't trust that boy, I don't

trust him at all!" she said, I could hear the slight pain in her voice.

I pursed my lips and looked away from her. I've already done so many bad things, how could I turn back now? "I'm sorry, ma, but I can't."

My mother looked down as she shook her head. "That's what Tyreek used to say," she looked up and had tears in her eyes. "Tyreek was always a rough kid, getting into fights left and right, but when he joined them Tyrants he was a copy of that man I used to love. I should have stopped him, I should have stopped both of you! Oh God, what have I done?" my mom said with her head in her hands. I didn't have the strength in me to console her this time. Did she always think of Ty as a mistake, the person I've looked up to since I was born?

"I don't want you hanging with that boy no more, at all!" she said, on the edge of bursting into a painful cry. I opened my mouth but before I could say anything she exclaimed, "He killed Tyreek, Sean, and he's gonna kill you too!"

"What?" My heart dropped.

"That boy is ruthless, Sean! He'll kill anyone without a second thought!" she exclaimed. I thought of

Dwayne's weird vibe earlier on his porch. Could she be right? No, mom was probably just in another stage of grief.

I nodded as we hugged, acting as if I believed her. But after that day I grew suspicious of Dwayne.

CHAPTER 9

My tense knuckles knocked on my hard plastic desk, making a beat as the class was receiving their tests. My math teacher handed me my algebra test face down and I was relieved to see an 89 marked on it.

I strayed away from drug dealing ever since I burned down Marco's stash house three weeks ago. I haven't met with Dwayne since that day, and at this point I was scared of what he'd do to me if I'd try to go back to him after all this time.

I looked across the classroom to see Devon grin with the test score he saw on his paper. Devon and I haven't talked since I told him I killed someone, and I could tell he was reluctant to even get near me.

Students immediately rushed out of their seats as the school bell rang, everyone ignoring the teacher's comments about homework due tomorrow. I left the classroom and went to my hallway locker.

As I was opening my locker in the crowded hallway, I followed my recent routine of stressing if Dwayne would try to take me from Rosewall High and hurt me. I never stressed about this when I was younger, but now it was like the cousin I knew wasn't there anymore. I knew he'd always been serious and cold with business, but after Tyreek's death he was different. I saw it in his unemotional eyes on the porch weeks ago.

I couldn't get my mom's words out of my mind: "He killed Tyreek and he's gonna kill you too!"

Suddenly I felt a mysterious presence behind me as a finger tapped my shoulder. I was startled and quickly turned around, only to see Ray with his backpack ready to go.

"You good?" asked Ray.

"Y-yeah, just startled me, that's all," I replied.

"Oh a'ight. Well, let's go to Fyre's corner store 'cuz a nigga starvin'," said Ray. With that, we went to the corner store. Ray and I have gotten closer since the funeral, and after hanging out with Ray more I realized that he wasn't that bad. We had put all of our beef aside and chilling with Ray made me realize why him and Ty were best friends, he was cool.

The real reason I started to hang out with Ray, though, was because he filled up the empty void of my brother. Ty's personality reflected in Ray, and I needed that. I needed some of that goofy energy, those funny jokes, and maybe even that protection. It pained me that my mom never saw that side of Tyreek.

Fyre's store was rather quiet, with no noise besides my hands rummaging through chip bags in the back of the store, trying to find a spicy one. The small bells on the old store door rang as two people entered. When I finally found the spicy chips I was searching for I looked up and peered from the back aisle to see Jason greeting Old Man Fyre. My heart dropped.

"Can I help you?" asked Fyre as Jason stepped up to the wooden counter.

"Yeah, I'm looking for Sean, where's he at?" asked Jason, looking around. I backed away from the edge of the aisle, evading his line of sight.

"Why would you want to know?" asked Fyre suspiciously.

"I need that little bastard now, where is he?"

"That boy ain't here right now," said Fyre.

"Damnit, old man, don't lie to me! I just saw him enter this store!" exclaimed Jason. I looked for any way to escape and I saw a dark backdoor across from me in my aisle.

"Yo, wassup, Jason?" I heard Ray say casually to Jason near the counter. I used the distraction and crept towards the backdoor. My hand lingered a few inches from the knob as I heard a loud smack from the counter.

"I'm not playin' with y'all, where is that bastard!?" exclaimed Jason. I could hear Ray's groans of pain on the floor, and then the sound of a shotgun being cocked and loaded.

"You better leave now!" exclaimed Fyre. My adrenaline kicked in as I quickly turned the knob and rushed out of the backdoor. But I thudded to the ground from the impact of running into a tall figure. I looked up and saw Dwayne staring down at me, occupying the exit.

Dwayne grabbed my arm and pulled me up. He forced me to the counter with one arm and pulled out a Glock from his pocket with the other. I desperately tried to pull my arm off him but his grip was too strong. We neared the counter and saw Ray on the ground and Jason held at gunpoint by Fyre.

Dwayne pointed his gun at Old Man Fyre and told him to put his shotgun away. Fyre slowly did as told, a sense of defeat in his face as Dwayne took me away to his car.

"Yo, Sergeant D, I'ma head home," said Jason when we got to the car. Dwayne nodded as he shoved me into the passenger seat. My body was very tense, contemplating the events that just happened. My body urged me to get out of the car and run, but Dwayne's Glock made me hesitate.

Dwayne got in the car and started driving. "So, you don't wanna be a Tyrant no more?" asked Dwayne.

"N-no, I do, it's just that I'm thinking about Tyreek, that's all," I lied. Tyreek was always in the back of my mind, but Dwayne was the real reason I hadn't been doing the Tyrant's errands.

"Hm… it won't matter anyway. I'ma handle this my damn self, I'ma be a real leader." Dwayne mumbled. My mind raced with questions of the words he just spoke. What did he mean, was he going to kick me out of the gang, was he going to stop having me help him with drugs?

The rest of the car ride was eerie, and the only sounds we could hear were the engines of cars on the road and occasional bumps from Dwayne's old tires. It was hard for me to comprehend what just happened at Fyre's, the fact that there was almost a shootout at the corner store made me dread how the police could get involved.

I was also scared of what Dwayne would do to me when we'd get to his house. Jason smacked Ray, the best boxer in Sacktown, so hard that he fell to the floor at Fyre's and groaned in pain, all for the sake of finding me. Dwayne wasn't scared to shoot Fyre either. If they were willing to do that to *get* me, what were they willing to do *to* me?

I had no more time to think or contemplate when Dwayne pulled into his driveway. My shaky legs acted like thin twigs as I followed Dwayne into his house and sat on the living room couch with him. "W-what's going on?" I asked, trying to make the situation less awkward.

Dwayne sighed "Look, Sean, in the beginning I only wanted an errand boy for me, someone who'd do my bidding and be serious, like a pawn," Dwayne said with a slight chuckle, I knew he wanted to say like Jason. "I never actually wanted another leader."

Dwayne's attitude changed and I looked at him with confusion.

"What do you mean? You pushed me to be a leader!"

"Shut the fuck up!" Dwyane yelled. I quivered a bit, and scooched away from Dwayne to the end of the couch. "I was the one who revived the Tyrants, I started the deals, I built up our wealth, I am the leader!" I stared at Dwayne in fear. "The Tyrants need me, not a sucka like you! And now you tryna leave the gang? You know too damn much, so... I gotta cut you off!"

Dwayne tried to grab me but I swiftly jumped off the couch and ran for my life. Dwayne didn't even bother to chase me as he shot at me with his pistol. I luckily dodged all of the bullets and ran down the hallway into Dwayne's room in time to lock the door. I pressed my back against it, hoping I could stop Dwayne from breaking it down.

A bullet fired through the door right next to my head, not allowing me to catch my breath. I hastily scrambled across the room as more bullets flew into the opposite wall. I retreated and stood on Dwayne's bed, there was no more shooting, but the past gunshots still echoed in my ears. I looked to the door and through the bullet holes I could see the shifting light of Dwayne behind it.

I wanted to cry, I wanted to wail, why was this happening? My own cousin was trying to kill me.

Before I knew it Dwayne busted down the door and pointed his gun at me, ready to shoot.

"Wait!" I exclaimed with my hands up as tears streamed down my face. "Wait…"

"What should I wait for, huh?" Dwayne said with a maniac smile. He motioned me to get down from the bed. I moved down, my back still against the wall and hands up. Dwayne pressed the barrel of his pistol against my forehead. "What, punk!?"

"W-well, I just want to know if…" I paused.

"If what!?" Dwayne exclaimed.

"If you killed Tyreek!" I shouted, bursting into tears. "D-did you kill my brother?"

Dwayne chuckled at my question, "Nah, Tyreek was cool. Why would I kill him?" I sniffled with a bit of relief. "It was prolly one of dem Sacker suckers," he said. Dwayne chuckled again, "You want to know who I did kill though?" I blinked twice for yes. "I killed your pops," he said.

I couldn't talk, I couldn't breathe, I couldn't feel. I was like that for five seconds, but it felt like five hours. "B-but, he's in prison!" I said in disbelief.

"Nah, I killed 'em, stabbed 'em four times," Dwayne said casually.

"How could you talk about it so calmly?" I said through my clenched teeth. My hands in the air balled up into fists, and I felt like punching his teeth out. But his gun was right in my face, loaded with bullets that could kill me in an instant.

"That's why your ma kicked me out at seventeen, 'cuz she knew what happened. If she told the police about it though, it'd be over for her. The Tyrants are ruthless, remember?" Dwayne said with a slick smile.

"You're psychotic! What happened to the old Dwayne, the one that I used to watch movies with and the one who showed love for me, what happened to him?" I asked. Dwayne paused.

"At Tyreek's funeral I cried in front of his casket. I was wonderin' if I did the right thing... but it didn't matter. I'm in too deep, there's no escape for me," he said with an awkward smile that seemed both wistful and evil. I wanted to tell him that it wasn't too late, that there was always a way out, but I just couldn't. Maybe he was in too deep with no escape; maybe it was the same for me. His smile disappeared. "Anyway, enough talkin', it's time for you to join your brother in Hell!"

Tears streamed down my face and my heart raced. Was this the end?

Suddenly there was a strong knock on the front door! "Open up! We have a warrant for arrest!" shouted a voice that sounded like the police.

A glimmer of hope had been shown as Dwayne was distracted. I quickly grabbed his pistol out of his hand and tried to Glock-whip him, but he was fast enough to block it.

I shot the pistol, trying to turn it and shoot his head, but he was too strong, and the grip he had on my other arm prevented me from punching him. After a couple of shots I stopped shooting and kneed Dwayne with all my strength into his stomach, he grunted in pain. With that, I ran to the door and turned around to point the gun at him. I pulled the trigger, but nothing happened, it was out of ammo!

"Open the door now!" the officer shouted.

As Dwayne was getting up, I threw the gun at him desperately and ran through the doorway. Dwayne chased after me through the hallway to the living room. It was like a game of tag, and at one point Dwayne caught me. He grabbed me by the shirt and held me up. All I could see was Sergeant D looking at me with a wrathful stare before he threw me to the floor with all his strength! I coughed up blood and wailed.

"You leave us no choice! We're breaking this door down!" the police officer shouted.

Dwayne continuously stomped on me and memories flooded my head of the Sackers, the Tyrants, Ray, Devon, even Tyreek. My life began to flash before my eyes.

"Three…" shouted the voice. "Two…" Dwayne became distracted so I kicked him in the groin from the ground and crawled to the nearest closet! "One!" The police broke down the door with a battering ram and saw Dwayne kneeling on the ground from pain.

"Hands up in the air, now!" one cop said. There were four cops, all of them with guns facing Dwayne. He put his hands up and two cops pushed him down to the floor. There was a vent grate in the closet door where I peeked through to see Dwayne's head on the ground, staring at me.

"Damnit, Sean!" he shouted as he vigorously wiggled around, trying to get the cops off him.

"Stop resisting!" one cop said, tightening Dwayne handcuffs. Dwayne grunted as the police took him away.

In that hollow closet I sobbed and cried, fear of the future hit harder than Dwayne did.

CHAPTER 10

I was panting heavily when I finally made it back to my apartment building. When the police were shoving Dwayne into their car I had snuck out the back door and ran for my life. Sweat covered my face as I trudged up the carpeted stairs to my apartment.

I had so many questions. Why did the police come? Did Dwayne really kill my dad? Has my mom been lying to me for all these years? How am I not dead? It was hard to think after miles of fearful nonstop running.

When I got home my mom was waiting for me on the couch. When she saw me, her face grew sympathetic and surprised. "Sean, baby, what happened to your face?" she said as she hastily went to the bedroom to get me some tissues. I confusedly wiped my face with the tissue she gave me, it was smeared with blood and sweat. I never noticed the scratches

Dwayne gave me in our fight. "What the hell happened out there, Sean?"

I tried to hold in my unexpected tears. "Dwayne, he did this to me," I answered as I sat on the couch with her. She consoled me, rubbing her arm on my sweaty back. "Then the police came and took him, so I ran all the way over here," I said, still panting a bit. I looked at my mom, but she was rather calm.

"Well, I'm just glad my baby's okay."

"You don't seem very surprised about the police being involved."

"Well, that's because I called 'em," my mom said with a slight grin on her face.

"But why? How'd you know I was in danger?" I asked as I blew my nose with another tissue.

"You didn't come home on time, and Fyre called me talkin' 'bout how Dwayne took you away and pulled a gun on him," she said.

"B-but what if the Tyrants find out, we'll be dead!"

"Don't worry, baby, they won't suspect your mama." When my mom said that I couldn't help but worry. What if the Tyrants did think that she and

Fyre snitched, or even me? I was the last person with Dwayne before he got arrested after all.

My mom saw me overthinking on the couch. "All right baby, it's time for you to get some rest, okay?" she was right, Dwayne beat the living crap out of me that day. However, I was still curious about what he told me.

"Ma, is dad... dead?" I asked hesitantly, part of me not wanting my mom to know that I was conscious of the secret.

My mom sighed. "D-Dwayne told you?" she said with an anxious frown.

"Why did you lie to me about dad being in prison for all these years, ma!?" I asked as my voice cracked. My beady eyes let tears flow down my face.

"Sean, I—" My mother couldn't find the apologetic words she was looking for until she managed to take a deep breath. "It was so hard when your dad died. I had so much fear about Dwayne trying to kill me too, that's when I turned to God and when you were arrested it just made me so scared and I noticed that you started to hang out with Dwayne more and —" A fresh rush of tears interrupted her words. "I just didn't want you to end up like Dwayne."

That statement left us in silence for a little while. I reflected on all of my past memories with Dwayne, and even with Tyreek. "Dad was just as funny as Ty, right?"

My mom smiled. "Yes, yes, he was."

Wrath, something that I tried to resist that past week.

Dwayne's words were always in the back of my head, his maniac smile constantly terrorizing my mind. My focus in school dwindled too. At least when Tyreek died I knew where my emotions were from. Now, I didn't know if my recent anger was from Dwayne, Tyreek, Devon, or even myself.

Whatever I was mad at, I couldn't deny that Dwayne had an effect. Even though I heard that he finally got locked up, I still didn't know how to feel about what he did. It was almost as if I hated and loved him at the same time, he was my cousin after all. I had spent so much time with him, even before joining the Tyrants.

But something was wrong with Dwayne. There was no way the real him would be ruthless towards his little cousin, right?

I couldn't shake the thought from my mind. Maybe Dwayne wasn't really who I thought he was. I didn't like it, but I realized that Dwayne didn't care if he was my cousin at all. He was a ruthless manipulator who had me work for him only to try and kill me later.

That didn't sit well with me, it almost gave me a feeling of worthlessness. I thought I was important for the Tyrants, that I was like a leader, but I was only a pawn in my cousin's scheme.

Even with Dwayne always in my head, I still felt that he wasn't where my anger was directly coming from. Maybe it was from the absence of my dad, my brother, Devon, maybe it wasn't anger at all. Maybe it was just loneliness.

I checked the clock in the living room as I laid on the couch. 8:30 PM and still mom hasn't come home. She's been at work since 6:00 AM and somehow we still didn't have enough money to buy cable for the month.

I huffed impatiently and rushed toward the bedroom to get some clothes on. Finally dressed for the cold night, I made my way to the place where I knew I could get involved with the Tyrants. There was nothing else I could do anyway, I didn't want to seem like a snitch and leave the gang for good. I'd have to encounter them one way or another.

Walking down the familiar route to the house, I felt my heart throb, as if it didn't want me to go and knock on CJ's door. I had no choice though. That thought of this being my only option was painful, but I knew it was true. Mom couldn't pay all those bills herself, and this seemed like the easiest way to get money.

I formed my shaky hand into a light fist as I knocked on CJ's door. I looked up at a big figure opening it. "Come in." CJ said.

Three months later, in May, the Tyrants gave me a big ego. I walked wherever I pleased with no fear of being jumped anymore, with the gun CJ had eventually given to me for gangbanging fueling my pride.

What I told the Tyrants wasn't something I was proud of, but it kept me alive. I didn't think they would believe my lie about Dwayne killing my brother so easily, especially since Dwayne called them from prison. Without Dwayne as a leader, the Tyrants were changing.

I had evolved with the Tyrants, since Marco's cartel was out of business, the gang turned to stealing, fighting, and gangbanging. It gave me the sense of dominance I've been looking for since the summer, but maybe that wasn't the best for me.

The beaming sun slowly began to fade as I made my way to Fyre's. I looked up at the warm colors filling the sky before I entered the store.

Fyre looked up from his sweeping when I came inside. Walking through the aisles of the store I decided to get some sour worms. Fyre quickly went through the transaction at the counter when I handed him my snack.

"No hi, no how are you?" I said, offended as Fyre abruptly handed me my bag.

"You know, Sean, I could have given you a job here. You didn't have to work with those hoodlums," said Fyre.

"What's dat 'posed to mean!?" I exclaimed.

"You gotta work on that temper, boy."

"Fuck off, you ain't my dad!"

Fyre sighed. "When I look in your eyes, I see that

killing instinct, that anger, a Tyrant's wrath. You don't wanna end up like your cousin, Sean. *You* might not know, but *I know* you're better than that."

Fyre's words made me pause. I then walked out of the store and ditched my sour worms, I wasn't hungry anymore.

I was on my way to Rosewall Park to observe the setting sun when I noticed someone familiar ahead of me. I approached him and said, "Ayo, where you from?"

The man turned around and I instantly realized who he was. It was the Sacker that caught me, the one with the beard and dark menacing eyes. It was him!

"I'm from here, nigga, what does it have to—" he stopped. "Wait a minute, ain't you that baby Tyrant I jumped back in the fall?" he asked with a slight smirk.

"I don't think I'll be such a baby when I shoot a hole through your body!" I said as I drew my gun and pointed it to his chest. He quickly put his hands up.

"Woah, a'ight, man, I'm sorry, okay. I won't come on your turf again, man, I'm sorry!" he pleaded.

"Were you sorry when you beat me half to death

with your crew and let me rot with the police!?" I yelled. Hot anger influenced my body and a voice in my head was telling me to pull the trigger, but Fyre's words made me hesitate.

The Sacker smacked the gun out of my hand when I hesitated and ran for his life. I quickly picked up my gun and chased him. He didn't give a damn about jaywalking as he made turns left and right and went through dozens of shortcuts. Finally, he made a turn into a long alley.

I pointed my gun at the Sacker and didn't hesitate to shoot this time. I pulled the trigger, but I missed. Instead, I hit… I looked closer to see Devon fall to the ground.

My body refused to move. Was this real? How could I miss? Devon was just trying to walk home, and he was shot. I ran over to Devon and looked down at him, the world around us faded away and all I could see was my best friend dying in my arms. Nothing could match the sharp pain of sorrow I felt when he looked me in the eyes.

"S-Sean? Wh-what hap—" he gagged and coughed out blood.

Why did I shoot? He was just trying to make it out

of this damned place! I wanted to say sorry, I wanted to reverse time, I wanted to keep Devon alive. The fatal bullet wound in his chest gushed out blood.

Devon gasped and struggled to breathe, his eyes slowly losing color. My vision went blurry with tears as I put my gun to his temple, I had to finish him. I sighed and looked at him one last time, he was too far gone to even understand what was happening.

"I'm sorry," I whispered. I only had the strength and time to say it once, but I wanted to repeat it a million times; that way there might have been a chance to be forgiven. With that I pulled the trigger and walked home, never looking back.

Fyre's words were true. I felt bitter, regretting what I've done. I figured this was what drove Dwayne crazy, this feeling of being trapped. This killing instinct, this wrath.

Maybe I could go and start a better life and make it out of Sacktown. But either way, these harsh moments of the Tyrants would always stay with me, lingering in my mind. It was as Tyreek always said, "Tyrant gang for life!"

EPILOGUE

We all have a purpose, and that purpose is based on fate. Fate is real. Fate is the choices we're given, and our life depends on what we do with those choices. Some make bad decisions, and some make good ones. What matters is the choices we have right now, not in the past, and not in the future, but now. Everyone's dealt a different hand, and whether we win or we lose, we always get a new hand of cards, a new situation in our lives, and look for a different opportunity. Now, our fate and purpose isn't luck based like cards, the different roads set for us are predetermined, and there's always a dead end. We never know what lies ahead of us, and what's behind us can only show us so much. But we always have choices presented to us until we reach the eventual end. Life is already hard enough, we can't let pressure or emotions block our destiny. Great lives are in reach if we manifest the destiny we want through our choices. It's ironic, because the only choice we really have is to keep moving forward.

[This epilogue is a short poem unrelated
to the story's perspective]

ABOUT THE AUTHOR:

Jordan Blaise lives in Mercer County, New Jersey, USA. He has been writing since he was able to read, and has loved it ever since. From poems to lyrics to opinionated essays to fictional stories, he does it all! In his free time he likes to write, work out, or devote time to God. As a 14 year old, he has had his fair share of anger issues growing up. He believes that there is hope for anyone to have what they feel is a better life, no matter the circumstances.

Official Website: jordanblaise.com

Official Instagram: @jbthewriter724

Made in the USA
Las Vegas, NV
15 June 2021

24790302R00069